My First Book

by Jane Belk Moncure
illustrated by Kathryn Hutton

THE CHILD'S WORLD

ELGIN, ILLINOIS 60120

Library of Congress Cataloging in Publication Data

Moncure, Jane Belk.
 My first book.

 (First steps to reading)
 Summary: Each illustration is accompanied by a
single word that identifies it.
 [1. Vocabulary] I. Hutton, Kathryn, ill.
II. Title. III. Series: Moncure, Jane Belk. First
steps to reading.
PZ7.M739Myfi 1984   [E]   84-17455
ISBN 0-89565-271-4

Distributed by Childrens Press, 5440 North Cumberland Avenue,
Chicago, Illinois 60656

CHILDRENS PRESS OFFERS
SEVERAL CARD PROGRAMS
FOR INFORMATION WRITE TO
CHILDRENS PRESS, CHICAGO, IL. 60607

My  First Book

eyes

nose

mouth

hair

feet

toes

Mommy

Daddy

hug

friends

balloons

16

hats

pajamas

bed

cup

plate

apple

cookies

ball

wagon

bear

doll

bunny

blocks

box